SOPHIE TROPHY TOO

Flashlights!
A new student!
How will Sophie handle
all the excitement?

SOPHIE TROPHY TOO   SOPHIE TROPHY

SOPHIE TROPHY TOO

SOPHIE TROPHY TOO

Eileen Holland
Illustrated by Brooke Kerrigan

Library and Archives Canada Cataloguing in Publication:
Title: Sophie Trophy too / Eileen Holland ; illustrated by Brooke Kerrigan.
Holland, Eileen, 1955- author. | Kerrigan, Brooke, illustrator.
Canadiana (print) 20190217340
Canadiana (ebook) 20190217359
ISBN 9781775351573 (softcover)
ISBN 9781775351597 (PDF)
ISBN 9781989724002 (HTML)
Classification: LCC PS8615.O4355 S68 2020 | DDC jC813/.6—dc23

Copy edited by Dawn Loewen
Proofread by Audrey McClellan
Cover and interior design by Julia Breese

Published by
Crwth Press
#204 – 2320 Woodland Drive
Vancouver, BC V5N 3P2
778-302-5525

Printed and bound in Canada on 100% post-consumer waste (PCW) paper.

MIX
Paper from
responsible sources
FSC® C016245

23 22 21 20 · 4 3 2 1

To my sister Frances,
who brings joy and laughter
to my life.

To my sister-in-law Linda,
whose delight in Sophie Trophy
warms my heart.

To my lovely daughter-in-law, Emily,
who has cheerfully embraced
Sophie's wild antics.

1
THE NOT-SHY-NOT-SCARED GIRL

Sophie raced to the covered area at Hilltop School, the November air nipping at her face. Monday morning and first in the Grade 3 lineup! Her best friends, Brayden and Enoli, joined her.

A high-pitched screech stabbed her ears. Jordy zombie-lurched down the line, arms spread, a toy airplane balanced on his nose. When it finally fell, he grabbed it, singing, "Woo-hoo! I did it. I did it."

1

Jordy caught her staring. "Don't try this. You're bad at balancing."

Sophie clenched her teeth. She wasn't good on the balance beam, but she had nose-balanced her toast last week. For ten whole seconds. *Not good at balancing? I'll show him*, she thought. Grinning, she fished inside her lunch bag.

The bell rang. Miss Ruby opened the door, her hair towering cotton-candy high. "Good morning, class. I have a surprise for you."

Warm air brushed Sophie's cheeks as the class trooped down the hallway to the classroom. *I love surprises.*

Behind her, Jordy was still bragging about his balancing skills. Sophie stopped in the cloakroom and twirled to face him.

With a banana hooked over her nose.

She waited for Jordy to freak out. Nothing.

No one else noticed either. Several kids breezed by to hang up their coats. The rest bunched up like grapes at the door.

"Who's that?" someone asked.

Hearing laughter close by, Sophie turned to see who was being so loud.

A tall, blond girl stood beside Miss Ruby. She was wearing a yellow ski jacket and abominable-snowman white boots. The girl looked at Sophie and her nose-banana and laughed again.

Sophie took the banana off her nose. *Is she laughing because nose-bananas are funny?* Sophie stiffened. *Or is she making fun of me?*

The girl said something to the kids hanging up their coats.

They all chuckled.

Even Miss Ruby. Like she was one of the girl's besties.

I was too shy to joke with anyone my first day here in September. Too scared.

The not-shy-not-scared girl gazed at Sophie again.

Cheeks burning, Sophie slipped the banana behind her back.

Slowly.

Without breathing.

When it was out of sight, she formed a tiny hole between her lips to suck in air. She lifted her chin high so the not-shy-not-scared girl wouldn't think Sophie was embarrassed. Her stomach felt like a brick was doing cartwheels in it.

"This is our new student, Hailey." Miss Ruby's bubbly voice filled the cloakroom. "Her family moved here yesterday."

"To be near my grandma. She needs our help."

Sophie's lower lip twitched. *Was Hailey's voice shaky?*

5

"Please make Hailey feel welcome." Miss Ruby glanced at the class with her I-care smile. "She'll need friends."

Sophie crammed her banana into her lunch bag. *Hailey isn't going to be friends with a banana-balancing clown. What I was doing wasn't even funny.* A grin jumped to her lips. *Well, maybe a bit funny.*

Miss Ruby clapped her hands. "Once you're all seated, I have another surprise."

Another one? Sophie chucked her coat and backpack onto her hook. She speed-walked to her seat. Where was Hailey sitting?

There she was. One row over and two seats back.

Miss Ruby had changed the seating to rows of double desks. Sophie frowned. Hailey was sitting next to Enoli, Sophie's best friend.

Once Miss Ruby was finished taking attendance, she walked to the back of the class.

Sophie heard metal rattling and bumping. She turned in her seat, curious-girl feelings fluttering inside her.

Miss Ruby was lifting a box.

With one foot raised on her chair, Sophie waited, watching her teacher walk up the aisle. Using superpower-toe-strength, she inched her body higher as Miss Ruby passed. She saw a flash of colours as she peered into the box.

Her other best friend, Brayden, sat at the desk beside Sophie. "What's in the box, Soph?" he asked.

She shrugged. "A rainbow?"

He snuffle-laughed. Sophie loved the sound. It was as if his nose thought she was funny.

Jordy yelped from across the aisle.

"Sophie peeked!"

Oh, no! Sophie lowered her toes until they lay pancake-flat on her seat.

Miss Ruby frowned. "Sophie, is it polite to steal a look?"

"No, it isn't. Sorry." *Miss Ruby's mad at me.* What about the new girl? Did she think Sophie was terrible for peeking?

Sophie couldn't control herself. She had to look.

Rising on her toes again, she leaned across to sneaky-eye-spy past Enoli.

Hailey stared back at her. She giggled, covering her mouth with her fingers.

Hailey's giggling made Sophie's raised-up superpower-toes weak and wobbly. She grabbed at her desk.

Too late!

She fell to the floor.

2
THE LEFT-OUT FEELING

Blushing, Sophie dragged herself off the classroom floor and into her seat.

"Are you okay?" Miss Ruby asked.

"Yes." *Except everyone's laughing and staring.*

She gazed straight ahead at a patch of chipped paint below the whiteboard. It looked like a bumblebee wearing a cowboy hat and eating a hot dog.

Miss Ruby smiled. "In two weeks, it's our turn to perform at the assembly."

Sophie liked assemblies. The students heard about upcoming events, and a class performed. She leaned forward. Her ears couldn't wait to hear more.

"We've watched a lunar eclipse and studied the sun's energy. So I found a song about the moon and the sun. As you sing, you'll do actions with these." Miss Ruby tipped the box so the students could see inside.

Everyone sucked in their breath. Mini-flashlights!

Red.

Yellow.

Green.

And royal blue.

Whispers criss-crossed the room.

Miss Ruby darkened the classroom. "Once you pick a flashlight, be careful not to shine it in anyone's eyes. Move it in different directions, making lines and shapes like this." She shone figure eights on the side wall with her grey flashlight, her hair puff jerking with every swoop. "Loop-de-loop, loop-de-loop, loop-de-loop!"

Everyone chuckled.

Miss Ruby was Sophie's best-teacher-ever. Like magic, she knew when Sophie needed help. Sophie loved Miss Ruby's I-care smile and her super-high hair puff. It seemed alive, like a pet she took with her everywhere.

Her teacher started to walk around the room, letting students choose a flashlight from the box.

"Everyone please take out your paper and pencils. Think up flashlight actions and write them down. You'll share your best action tomorrow. Why might we keep flashlights at home?"

Brayden raised his hand. "For emergencies and stuff, like the power going off."

Sophie grinned at the class. "Or to find long-lost treasure in your attic!"

Everyone laughed, especially Hailey.

Sophie's eyebrows hippity-hopped. *That kid laughs a lot. I like that.* Maybe Hailey could be her friend. Sophie glanced at her. Hailey didn't dress like Sophie, or act shy or scared. Even on her first day. *Nope. We're too different.*

Jordy jumped up. "If there are extras, can I have two?"

"In your seat. There aren't any extras."

"Aww." Jordy flopped back down.

Miss Ruby's face brightened. "One more thing. I made a giant moon mask and a puffy sun costume. Tomorrow I'll pick one student to play the moon and another to play the sun."

Sophie imagined herself as the sun, wearing yellow and covered in sunrays. Glowing.

"You're dreaming, Sophie," Miss Ruby commented. "Everyone's listing flash-light actions."

Sophie nodded. She started her list.

"I want yellow," Hailey said.

"I do, too." Enoli smiled at Hailey.

What? Enoli's favourite colour is green. Does she want yellow because Hailey does? Watching them, Sophie got a left-out feeling. Enoli was super-quiet, except when she learned something interesting. Then she chattered endlessly. Would she talk more with Hailey than she did with Sophie?

Think about colours instead. Sophie pictured the royal-blue party dress Auntie Pop-Pop had given her.

Queens and princesses wear royal-blue dresses.

And royal-blue capes.

And royal-blue jewels.

And use royal-blue flashlights.

"I want royal blue," cried Sophie.

Neither girl looked her way. Sophie sighed.

Jordy chose his flashlight, then waited until Miss Ruby moved away. "Look, Sophie. I got royal blue. You'll be last to pick because you're by the window. You won't even get a choice."

Sophie wolf-snarled at him.

By the time Miss Ruby reached Brayden, there were two flashlights left. "I know you want blue, Soph, so I'll take green."

"Really?"

"Yeah." Brayden smiled.

"Thanks." Swivelling sideways, Sophie grabbed the flashlight and clicked it on.

Nothing happened.

She shook it. Smashed lightbulb bits and cracked lens pieces fell to the floor.

Her lip quivered. "Aww!"

Brayden frowned. "Is it wrecked, Soph?"

"Yes."

"Ha ha," cried Jordy.

Hailey and Enoli looked at Sophie with sad eyes.

Miss Ruby swept up the smashed bits and collected Sophie's broken flashlight. An I-care smile crossed her face. "I have a mini-flashlight in my car you can use."

Sophie tried to smile. Her mouth had a hard time turning upward.

"Do you have your own flashlight at home, Sophie?"

"Yes, for camping. Plus one a firefighter gave me at the Teddy Bear Picnic."

Miss Ruby's eyes danced. "Wonderful."

"And a headlamp—a flashlight you wear on your forehead."

Sophie remembered her excitement when her dad and Uncle Ray bought headlamps for themselves, Auntie Pop-Pop, and Sophie.

Do queens wear royal-blue headlamps?
During castle emergencies?

"Sophie?" Brayden said. "Your headlamp sounds like fun."

She blinked. She shouldn't be dreaming. Not with Miss Ruby nearby. "It is fun. I also have a zebra flashlight and one shaped like a cookie."

Everyone near Sophie laughed.

She frowned. *My flashlights aren't funny. Why do I always get laughed at?*

Hailey caught her eye. "I'd like to see your flashlights."

Sophie's gloomy-girl feelings floated away like a cloud off a mountain.

"It's almost recess, class," said Miss Ruby. "You are responsible for keeping your flashlight in a safe spot until the assembly. Your desk is best."

She turned to Sophie.

"Can you bring your collection for Show and Tell on Friday?"

"Yes."

Hailey smiled. "Don't forget your cookie flashlight."

"I won't," Sophie promised. Could Hailey become her friend after all?

Enoli's face lit up. "I want to see that one, too, Hailey."

Sophie silent-snorted inside her head. *Shouldn't she be telling me that?*

Glancing at the boys seated near him, Jordy grinned. "If we all fall down a giant bunny hole, Sophie Trophy can rescue us with her dumb cookie flashlight!" The boys burst out laughing.

What's dumb is Jordy's nickname for me. And the way Enoli does what Hailey does.

3
WHY ARE YOU HERE?

After recess, Miss Ruby brought Sophie the mini-flashlight from her car.

"It's turquoise!" Sophie felt the room spin. Was colour-dizzy a thing?

"It's beautiful," whispered Enoli.

Brayden gasped. "Yeah, it is."

Hailey joined them. "Wow. Awesome colour."

"I know. Thank you, Miss Ruby."

"You're welcome."

The room became noisy as the students took their seats.

The flashlight reminded Sophie of her aunt and uncle's trip to Mexico. Auntie Pop-Pop brought home seashells for Sophie and a turquoise ring for herself. *And* a tan.

She had let Sophie wear her ring. It was a triangle of turquoise beauty.

When Auntie Pop-Pop had asked her to give the ring back, Sophie's fingers couldn't do it.

Not until Dad did the high-eyebrow lift.

Now she had the same problem. When she tried to put her flashlight in her desk, Sophie's fingers couldn't do it.

Miss Ruby had said to keep it in a safe spot. Sophie slipped it in her pocket.

***

Sophie's head spun as she completed a page on adding big numbers. "Numbers shouldn't be allowed to be this long."

"I know," Brayden muttered.

She asked to use the hall fountain. As she finished drinking, Sophie saw a sick girl leaving the medical room with her mother. *That room's always dark!* She walked perfect-student slowly past the office, then knee-surfed into the medical room.

Across the room was a half-shut door leading to the office. *Tappity-tap!* Ms. Babette was secretary speedy-typing.

Ms. Babette won't notice me. For a quick minute.

She shut the hall door. The room darkened. Kneeling on the bed's snow-white sheet and cozy blanket, she flicked on her flashlight. It lit up the bandages and gauze in the medicine cabinet windows.

She wished she had a sore arm so someone could wrap it in soft, white gauze. The class would feel sorry for her if she returned with a wrapped-up arm.

She zigzagged the beam along the floor. It looked like a soccer ball being kicked around cones. A flashlight was better than a wrapped-up arm.

Behind the half-shut door, a deep voice asked, "Did Emma go home?"

"Yes. I must straighten up the medical room." Ms. Babette's chair made a rolling sound.

She's coming!

As Sophie leaped off the bed, her foot snagged on the snow-white sheet. She tumbled to the floor, dragging the sheet and pillow with her.

Sophie hid her face in the pillow and stayed as still as a statue. She wished she was a statue. Statues didn't get in trouble for playing with flashlights in medical rooms.

Ms. Babette click-clacked in. The light flicked on. "Emma? Why are you on the floor? I thought you went home."

Sophie sat up. "I'm not Emma."

"Oh, Sophie. Why are you here?"

Heavy footsteps clomped up behind her. "And what's that shining under the sheet?"

Sophie sighed. If only she could hide inside the pillow where it was all fluffy and friendly. She switched off her flashlight. Pushing aside the sheet, she stood up.

"I'll let you two talk." Ms. Babette left.

The principal's eyebrows bunched together. "Feeling sick, Sophie?"

"No, Mr. Homework." Sophie moaned. "Sorry. I keep forgetting your real name is Mr. *Homewood.*"

"Hmm. Everyone forgets names. Why are you here?"

"Miss Ruby gave us flashlights for song actions, only mine was broken. Now I have this beautiful turquoise one." Smiling, Sophie held it up.

Mr. Homework didn't look excited about turquoise.

She gulped. "I didn't get to use my broken flashlight, so I came in to try this one. For a teeny-tiny second."

He sighed. "Sophie, no more visits to the medical room."

She frowned. "What if I have a scratchy throat or a sneezing problem or a tummy bug?"

Mr. Homework's mouth turned serious-principal flat. "Scratchy, sneezy, and buggy problems are good reasons to come here. Flashlights are not. Back to class."

***

After eating lunch, Sophie and Hailey helped Miss Ruby get the paint ready for art class.

Cleaning up in the washroom afterward, Hailey asked, "Is Sophie Trophy your real name?"

Sophie dried her hands. "No, that's a nickname Jordy made up to tease me."

"Ohh."

"He teased Safiya, too, for being sick again."

"Poor Safiya."

Sophie nodded. "Safiya said her throat hurt. She had white patches at the back of her mouth."

Hailey shuddered. "That's awful."

Sophie pulled her flashlight out of her pocket. Flicking it on, she giggled. "Can you check if I have any patches?"

Grinning, Hailey took the flashlight and shone it inside Sophie's mouth. "Nothing. Check mine."

Taking the flashlight, Sophie lit up Hailey's throat. "Nope." A thought spun forward, bringing a smile to her lips. "But there is a little man hanging from that dangly skin at the back of your mouth."

"Noooo!"

"Yes. He's wearing a pointy green hat."

Hailey slapped the wall, laughing.

Sophie giggled. "He waved at me."

Laughing harder, Hailey slapped the wall again. "You're so funny."

"What's all the noise?" boomed a voice.

They froze.

"Come out, please."

Shoulders tingling, Sophie led Hailey into the hallway.

Mr. Homework stood there. "Oh, it's you, Hailey. You girls should be outside.

"Why are you here?"

"After getting the paint ready for Miss Ruby—"

Sophie cut in, waving her flashlight. "We were checking each other's throats. To have healthy health. And hooray, hooray! No white patches." She felt a giggle rising. "Just a little man in a pointy green hat."

Mr. Homework's face scrunched up. "That's silly talk, Sophie. And that flashlight should only be used for practising actions."

The end-of-lunch bell rang.

"Off you go."

Hailey was quiet as they walked down the hall.

Sophie had a sad heart. *We were having so much fun. The way friends do. But I guess a real friend would have let Hailey finish explaining.*

4
THE NEVER-EVER-EVER FRIEND BRIDGE

After lunch, Sophie's class carried clipboards, paper, and pencils to the park beside the school.

Miss Ruby pointed at a maple tree reaching overhead. A gust of wind shook the tree's branches, and orange leaves fluttered down. "Half the class will draw this tree from across the meadow. The other half will draw it from the base of the trunk. The drawings will be wonderfully different!"

The class chattered excitedly.

"Straight up the trunk. Please, please, please," whispered Sophie, her chest fluttery.

Half hiding her smile behind her fingertips, Enoli nodded. Brayden grinned.

Hailey stood nearby, chattering with some girls. Was she upset about their talk with the principal?

Miss Ruby clapped to catch everyone's attention. The curls in her hair puff fluttered in the breeze, like tiny hands waving at Sophie.

Sophie's fingers twitched, wanting to wave back.

"Remember," Miss Ruby said. "Draw the tree higher up the paper if it's farther away. Draw it lower if it's close."

Sophie, Enoli, Brayden, and Hailey were

picked for the tree trunk group. Jordy stalked across the meadow wearing a crabby-critter face.

They stared up the tree.

"I feel dizzy," Enoli said.

"That's because the tree's swaying." Sophie flung her arms around the maple. "What a strong, beautiful trunk. I love you, Mr. Tree!"

Enoli and Brayden chuckled.

Hailey peeked around the tree at them, then disappeared.

They drew quietly. As they finished, Sophie noticed a dark hole in the tree trunk. She tugged out her flashlight, clicked it on, and shone it into the hole. "You guys, there's an animal in there."

Enoli shrank back.

Brayden stepped over for a look. Hailey scooted around the tree and peered over his shoulder. "What big eyes," she said.

"They really are huge," Sophie whisper-screeched. "Like moose eyes."

"A moose couldn't fit in there." Brayden let out a snuffly laugh.

She tried to keep from giggling. "It could if it did Auntie Pop-Pop's twisty-bendy yoga. *And* folded up its antlers."

"Folding antlers?" Brayden yelped.

Hailey laughed. "It would have to fold them fifty times to squish in there."

"And fold its legs and sticky-outie moose muzzle, too," added Sophie.

They all giggled.

"I'm scared." Enoli hugged herself tightly. "Check again."

"Okay." Sophie lit up the hole, then flicked her flashlight off. "They're not eyes. They're mushrooms."

"Whaaat?" Brayden's eyelids drooped.

Pretend-trembling, Sophie backed away. "Danger, danger! There's a mushroom-eyed maple monster in there, waiting to attack."

Brayden, Enoli, and Hailey dove behind Sophie, squealing.

The other group returned from the meadow. Miss Ruby's voice rang out. "Painting time! Line up at the door."

Everyone charged up the path to the school. Sophie arrived at the door first with Hailey close behind.

At the door, Sophie turned to talk to her. Hailey was laughing with Enoli. Sophie huffed.

They're always together.

Moments later, the class was inside, hanging up coats and grabbing paint-brushes. They knelt on the floor beside large sheets of paper to paint their trees.

Sophie gazed sideways, admiring the ridges on Hailey's tree trunk.

"To show that the tree's closer, make

it darker," said Miss Ruby. "To show that it's farther away, make it lighter."

Sophie swished extra paint up her tree trunk.

And extra, extra paint.

And one last layer.

And another.

Then another. "Six layers should be enough."

Brayden glanced over. "That's thick."

"I'll stop. It's getting sloshy." Sophie loaded paint onto her brush. Balancing on one hand, she leaned over the painting to splotch leaves on her tree. "These little guys are hard because I can barely reach—"

With her hand close to the soggy trunk, the paper tore. Sophie fell forward, face-planting into her tree trunk.

All.

Six.

Goopy.

Layers.

Miss Ruby and the class gasped.

Sophie dropped her paintbrush. As she pushed herself up, Jordy hooted loudly.

There was paint in her hair and paint on her cheeks.

She even had paint on her teeth.

Using a Dracula voice, Jordy wailed, "The monster rises from the swamp."

She rocked back onto her knees, paint dribbling everywhere. "My nose. It's dripping off my face!"

"It's what?" Miss Ruby hurried away. "I'll get a wet cloth."

Sophie finger-flicked paint off her cheeks.

"Stop it," Hailey howled. "You're splattering me!"

"Sorry." As Sophie leaned backward, her left hand landed in the tub of brown

35

paint. Her right hand tipped over the orange paint. It streamed across the floor. "Hailey, get away, get away! It's coming."

Hailey glanced at Sophie. "What is?"

"The orange."

"From your lunch?" Hailey stared at her again.

"No, look *down*."

The orange paint splashed Hailey's abominable-snowman-white boots. Hailey jumped up, shrieking. Grabbing their paintings, her classmates backed away.

Sophie stood up. Dashing forward to help, she slipped in the paint. Sophie crashed into Hailey and fell, her forehead smacking the floor.

There was a girl-in-danger wail.

Then a thud.

Sophie lifted her face. On her right, she saw paint-splattered arms.

On her left, she saw white and orange boots.

Hailey was on both sides of her at once. And above her, like a never-ever-ever friend bridge.

Sophie slithered out from under her, right over Hailey's painting.

She ripped it in half.

Hailey glared at her. "You ruined my painting! How could you?"

5
SOUR-FACED SOPHIE

The next morning, a red-faced Sophie crept to the back of the class lineup.

Sneaky-eye spying, she saw Hailey joking with Enoli and Brayden up ahead. Hailey, who would never be her truly-true friend. Not after yesterday.

Sophie tightened her grip on her backpack strap as Miss Ruby led them inside. Would Brayden and Enoli start liking Hailey *more* than her?

Probably.

Hailey wouldn't nose-balance bananas.

Or peek at teacher surprises.

Or face-plant in goopy tree trunks.

Sophie hung up her coat and backpack. She walked to her seat past staring eyes. *At least I still have my little turquoise friend.*

"Let's talk about song actions." Miss Ruby lowered the blinds. "Bring your flashlights to the carpet, please. Jordy's row first."

When Sophie reached the carpet, she plunked down behind Hailey and Enoli. Their whispering made her ears cranky. *I should be with Enoli. Hailey hardly knows her.*

Miss Ruby smiled. "What's your flashlight action, Jordy?"

"Circles." Jordy twirled his flashlight, his head looping around with it.

The class laughed.

Miss Ruby recorded his idea on the whiteboard. "Brayden, you're next."

He bit back a grin. "When the moon actor's onstage, can we shine our flashlights under our chins?"

"Let's try it." Miss Ruby turned off several lights. When everyone held their lit flashlights under their chins, excited screeching bounced against the windows.

"You're scary. The audience will love it!" said Miss Ruby. "What's your idea, Hailey?"

"Waving wiggly sunrays above our heads."

"Nice."

The boy beside Sophie spoke. He suggested they blink their flashlights like twinkling stars while singing about a starry night.

She grinned. She'd blink her flashlight all day long.

Why not get started? Sophie pushed the *on* button at the back of her flash-light with her thumb.

Ten, twenty, thirty times.

Her heart jiggled with joy. Like it did standing in line for mini-doughnuts at the summer fair. Or jumping into a bumper car.

When her thumbs became tired, she tried chin-blinking.

Ouch. Her chin was so bony.

Wait! How about elbow-blinking?

It worked. But when Sophie stopped to change elbows, the clicking continued. And it got louder, like crickets at sunset.

"Class, that's enough," said Miss Ruby. "Class!"

Sophie glanced up, startled.

Every student was elbow-blinking and grinning at Sophie.

She got a proud-heart feeling. She would

have grinned back. Except Miss Ruby was her best-teacher-ever.

Sophie flicked off her flashlight. So did her classmates.

Miss Ruby's smile returned. "Thank you. Sophie, Queen of the Blinkers, what is your best action?"

"I have twenty-two best actions!"

"Let's hear your favourite."

"My best-best action is holding our flashlights against our hearts. When we sing about our friend, the sun."

Miss Ruby's eyes sparkled. "That's beautiful."

Sophie beamed.

The rest of the students shared their ideas, Enoli last.

Her face glowed. "I researched the moon. In the fall, it stays low on the horizon. It looks orange because air molecules in the atmosphere scatter green, blue, and purple light away. That leaves behind yellow, orange, and red light. Pollution also makes the moon look orange."

"Wonderful research, Enoli." Miss Ruby smiled.

"Thanks. Can we poke mini-flashlights wrapped in orange tissue paper through the moon mask? So it glows orange?"

"Of course."

Hailey nudged Enoli. "That'll look spooky."

I would have said that. If I wasn't back here.

Jordy cackled. "Grampa says the moon's orange because it's made of cheese!"

Giggles ran races around the carpet.

Miss Ruby switched on the lights. "Enoli mentioned pollution. What should we do with our dead flashlight batteries?"

"Recycle them," Brayden said.

"Or use rechargeable batteries," said Sophie. "The ones in our flashlights can be used over and over and over and over—"

"That's enough overs," Miss Ruby said. "Now, who'd like to be the moon?"

I'll wait. Sophie's heart thumped. *I'd rather be the sun.*

Several students made moon faces. Rising to his knees, Jordy bugged out his eyes and froze, a toothy grin on his face.

"You're our moon, Jordy."

"Yes!" Jordy pumped his fists.

"Now, the sun. Let's see peaceful, shining faces."

Smiling, Sophie fluttered her eyelashes and swayed her arms like sunrays.

So did half the class.

"You're all excellent," Miss Ruby said, "but I'm going to choose …"

Sophie heard her name called.

She jumped up, waving sunray arms and giving the class light. And a quick view of her turquoise flashlight.

Jordy laughed. "She said *Safiya*, not *Sophie.*"

"I'm sorry, Sophie." Miss Ruby bit her lip. "Jordy's right."

Sophie glanced at Safiya, frowning. Safiya was smiling, her hands pressed against her cheeks. When she saw Sophie's face, her smile faded.

The recess bell rang. Sophie bolted outside and huddled against the wall.

Brayden joined her. "Safiya's name sounds like yours, Soph."

"I know." Sophie blinked back tears. Noticing Hailey peeking at her from around the corner, Sophie turned away.

Enoli brought Sophie her coat. "I wish you were the sun."

"Thanks."

Sophie's chest ached as she put her coat on.

She was sad she didn't get the part.

And because she stared at Safiya with a sour face. Safiya was nice. And she was sick a lot. A kind person wouldn't frown at Safiya. Not when Safiya needed to be the sun more than anyone.

6

SNORTY-SNIFFING AND SHADOW PUPPETS

On Friday, the class gathered on the carpet for Show and Tell.

The first speaker sat on a chair beside Miss Ruby. He talked about scoring a goal in his hockey game.

Sophie was next up with her flash-light collection. The class smiled at her zebra flashlight, then laughed at her cookie flashlight.

She pulled on her headlamp and swished her fingers past it. The light flicked on.

"Aww," Jordy said. "I want one of those."

"I wish I'd had a headlamp when I was young," said Miss Ruby.

Sophie pictured Miss Ruby teaching with four headlamps on her hair puff. Every kid would pay attention.

A girl raised her hand. "Sophie's headlamp would go great with Safiya's costume."

Everyone looked Sophie's way. Her throat tightened.

Then she noticed Miss Ruby's I-care smile. "May Safiya borrow it?"

Kind words pushed forward inside Sophie. "Of course."

Safiya beamed at her. Enoli and Brayden smiled, too.

Sophie smiled back. Grabbing her flash-lights, she lowered herself to the carpet.

Last up for Show and Tell was Hailey. Joining Miss Ruby, she gently lifted a plant out of a box. "Grandma's Christmas cactus has been covered in buds for weeks. Its first flower just opened."

The bloom bowed toward Sophie, heavy with petals.

It looked like a pink swan or the place a fairy would sleep in a magic garden.

It was perfect. And so close.

Reaching out, Sophie stroked the petals. Her eyelids drooped. *Oh, that's the most softly-soft softness. Like puppy ears. Or fuzzy mittens. Or marshmallows.*

"It's fragile, Sophie," warned Miss Ruby.

Snap! The bloom fell to the floor.

A chill roller-coastered up one of Sophie's arms and down the other.

Her classmates groaned.

"Dear me," Miss Ruby said.

Hailey's shoulders turned ladder-stiff. "You wrecked it."

Sophie had a sad heart. "I'm really sorry."

Hailey's lips trembled. She put the cactus back in the box.

***

Miss Ruby shivered as the class returned from practising the song onstage that afternoon. "Brr! I shouldn't have left my sweater in the staff room."

Being helpful would make Sophie feel better after snapping off the bloom.

She raised her hand. "I'll go get it."

"Oh, thank you."

Sophie had curious-girl feelings as she

walked down the hallway. Whenever she passed the staff room at lunchtime, she heard teachers laughing. What were they doing in there? Telling knock-knock jokes? Playing Twister?

Stepping into the staff room, she shut the door.

There were many tables and chairs, so no room for Twister.

Boring grown-up papers covered the walls instead of art and autumn leaves. Sophie felt sorry for the teachers.

One table had a card on it from a moving-away family.

There were flowers.

And chocolates.

There were three chocolates left in the box. "Cherry. My favourite." Leaning over, Sophie snorty-sniffed it. Oh, the chocolatey sweetness! Drool rimmed her lips, threatening to spill over. "You other

53

chocolates look good, too," she added, to keep from hurting their feelings.

She blinked. *Miss Ruby's sweater.* Sophie rushed to the closet. As she spotted the sweater, she noticed the closet was dark. Shadow-puppet dark!

Sophie grabbed her flashlight and clicked it on. She wedged it between the thin shelf overhead and the ledge it sat on. When she shoved the coats back, the light glowed on the far wall.

She pulled the double doors shut.

Too scary.

She opened them halfway.

Sophie froze. Mr. Homework had said her flashlight was to be used only for actions. *Aren't shadow puppets actions?*

Making a fist, then raising two fingers for ears, she hopped a friendly bunny across the flashlight beam.

The flying bird was next. With palms

facing her, Sophie spread her fingers and crossed her wrists. Hooking one thumb around the other, she moved her fingers and thumbs. Like wings and a beak. *Brayden and Enoli would love my bird. Would Hailey? Not today.*

She was making reindeer antlers when she heard click-clacking in the hallway. Sophie pulled her flashlight down, flicked it off, and hid behind the coats.

The staff room door opened. "Caramel truffle time," whispered a voice.

Sophie's eyebrows rose high-jumper high.

Ms. Babette!

7
LEGS IN THE CLOSET!

Sophie stood hockey-stick-stiffly in the staff room closet. She peeked out between Miss Ruby's hedgehog sweater and a peppermint-green raincoat.

"There's my little friend," purred Ms. Babette as she picked up a chocolate.

As she watched Ms. Babette, Sophie realized something.

She wasn't well hidden.

Not.

At.

All.

Her legs and feet showed below the coats.

Ms. Babette turned, dabbing at her lips. Peering toward the coats, she froze. "Legs in the closet! Who's in there? Pop on out. Chop, chop."

Sophie slipped her flashlight into her pocket.

The flashlight was lucky. It had somewhere to hide. And no legs to get it into trouble.

Sophie wriggled out between the sweater and the raincoat.

Ms. Babette jerked backward. "Sophie? Why are you here?"

"I'm getting Miss Ruby's sweater."

Ms. Babette crossed her arms. "Then why is it still in the closet?"

Sophie's lips squirmed. "I was making shadow puppets."

"After playing with your flashlight in the medical room? You need another talk with the principal."

Sighing, Sophie grabbed the sweater. She followed Ms. Babette.

***

Tick. Tick. Tick.

The office clock scolded Sophie.

Loudly.

Angrily.

Tick. Tick. Tick.

She glared at it.

Dead batteries. That's what that clock needs.

Bang! Clitter-clatter. Things rolled and dropped to the floor.

"How clumsy of me." Ms. Babette disappeared. "Ouch. My knees," she said, letting out a raspy groan. Her chair rattled as she pulled herself into it again.

Whipping out her flashlight, Sophie stopped to admire its turquoise beauty. Then she dove under the desk.

Ms. Babette's chair rolled backward. "Sophie, I thought a wild animal was attacking my legs."

"Nope, just me keeping your knees from hurting." Sophie clicked her flashlight on. Fuzzy ribbons of dust coated the tangled cords. Pens stuck out of them like rockets ready to fly to the moon.

"What a thoughtful, kind-hearted girl," gushed Ms. Babette.

Thoughtful. Kind-hearted. If only Hailey had heard Ms. Babette calling her that. She handed up a fistful of pens.

"You angel!"

Grinning, Sophie tummy-slid backward past the chair.

Her feet smacked into something.

White running shoes with blue jogging pants above?

Mr. Homework! With his unhappy-principal frown. "Using your flashlight again, Sophie?"

"Yes." She stood up. "Because of Ms. Babette's knees."

"What?"

"They fell under her desk."

Mr. Homework rubbed his forehead. "Her knees fell under her desk?"

"No, my pens did," explained Ms. Babette. "What a helpful girl, getting them for me."

"Hmm. But why is Sophie here?"

Ms. Babette cleared her throat. "She was making shadow puppets in the staff room closet."

Mr. Homework raised his eyebrows. All five of his forehead wrinkles rose too.

Lifting her eyebrows, Sophie touched her own forehead.

No wrinkles.

She would check again when she got to middle school.

"After I found Miss Ruby's sweater, I made shadow puppets," explained Sophie. "For a teensy second." Sophie stopped. *Hailey would have taken the sweater straight back.*

Sophie pulled it off her chair. "Miss Ruby's cold. She needs her sweater."

"You should have thought of that sooner. Let's go."

The principal was walking her back to class!

Her legs felt like jiggly-jelly.

Strawberry, lemon, raspberry ...

Forget the jelly flavours.

At the classroom, Jordy squawked, "Sophie's back."

Sophie handed the sweater to Miss Ruby. As she sat down, she heard principal-mumbling.

When Mr. Homework left, Miss Ruby called Sophie's name.

As she got up to go to Miss Ruby's desk, Sophie's cheeks burned.

"Is she in trouble?" asked Hailey.

Enoli shrugged. "I hope not."

Sophie got a warm feeling about Enoli. Then her happiness faded. *Enoli hasn't talked to me much since Hailey arrived.*

Miss Ruby had the no-smile face. "You've been searching for dark places to use your flashlight. May I have it, please?"

Sophie's stomach pretzel-twisted. She should have brought the sweater to Miss Ruby instead of making shadow puppets. Then the kids wouldn't be whispering about her.

She returned to her seat.
Without her flashlight.

8

THE SHY-SCARED GIRL

The next week at school, Sophie used the turquoise flashlight only to practice song actions for the first three days.

On the fourth day, Miss Ruby gave it back. She led the class onstage. "This is your last practice before tomorrow's assembly. Choose a partner and work on your chorus actions. Then we'll run through the whole song."

Sophie looked at Hailey. Just as Hailey and Enoli grabbed each other's hands.

Sophie's head spun like socks in a dryer. *I don't blame Hailey. Things go wrong when I'm around. But Enoli didn't even look for me.*

Then Brayden shuffled onstage.

"Hey, Brayden, do you want to practise the chorus together?"

He grinned. "Yeah, sure."

Hearing Brayden's friendly voice was like biting into a slice of Auntie Pop-Pop's homemade bread, fresh from the oven and thick with strawberry jam—the lumpy kind.

Wait a minute. Brayden came in late. He had to be my partner.

Sophie's head felt bowling-ball heavy.

So did her heart.

***

At lunchtime, Hailey pulled on her yellow jacket and red and yellow scarf. She left with her mom.

When Sophie took her seat after lunch, voices buzzed in the cloakroom.

She tucked her hair back and cupped her hands behind her ears to super-ear hear what was being said.

It didn't help.

Miss Ruby entered the classroom. Hailey trailed in behind her, wearing red glasses with yellow hearts at the corners.

Several students told Hailey they liked her glasses. Hailey blushed.

All through social studies, Hailey twisted her bracelet around and around her wrist. She hardly looked up.

Brayden met Sophie and Enoli at the pencil sharpener. "Hailey's shy about her glasses. I heard her outside asking her mom to walk her into class."

"Really?" asked Sophie.

He nodded. "But her mom had to help her grandma."

Poor Hailey. "She shouldn't feel shy," said Sophie. "Lots of kids have glasses. I love Safiya's green ones. They're the colour of kiwis and limes. It's like she's wearing fruit on her face. My mouth gets drooly just looking at her glasses."

Brayden laughed. "You *should* get a trophy, Sophie, for the funny things you say."

She grinned.

***

When the bell rang, Miss Ruby stood at the door giving last-minute reminders.

"Wait for me?" Sophie asked Enoli and Brayden.

They nodded.

She stepped over to Hailey's desk. "I like your glasses. Red and yellow are your best colours."

Hailey looked up. "Thanks."

Sophie handed her a letter. "Um, I wrote this I'm-sorry letter for your grandma, about the cactus."

A smile flickered on Hailey's lips. "She likes letters."

Sophie blinked. *Is Hailey being nice because Enoli and Brayden are watching?* "My grandma does, too," said Sophie. "She keeps her friends' cards for months. If they have cute animals on them, she keeps them even—"

"Blaah!" Jordy jumped in front of Sophie with a banana peel spread over his face.

"Gack!" Springing sideways, Sophie smacked Hailey's shoulder.

Knocking her to the floor.

Jordy raced off laughing.

"I'm sorry." Sophie reached out to pull Hailey up.

Ignoring Sophie's outstretched hand, Hailey got to her feet. She grabbed her homework and left.

"I keep not-on-purpose messing up." Sophie's shoulders drooped.

Enoli and Brayden shook their heads, wearing sad-kid faces.

Looking at them, Sophie felt her own face sag.

Except her nose, because people noses couldn't sag. Only elephant noses could.

Did Enoli and Brayden feel sorry for Sophie? Or were they sad because of how Sophie acted? She knocked Hailey over, didn't she?

Sophie sighed. She was pretty sure she felt her nose sagging now, too.

9

SOPHIE THE TORNADO

Friday morning, Sophie trudged up the steep sidewalk to Hilltop School.

As she joined Brayden and Enoli, Hailey walked toward them clutching her flashlight. *Is she still upset that I knocked her over?*

"Hi, Enoli," Hailey cried. As she lifted her hand to wave, the flashlight flew out of her fingers.

Sophie gasped. She leaped basketball-player high to catch it.

Ping! The flashlight bounced off the tippity-top tip of Sophie's finger and flew into the street. There was a grinding sound as Jordy's dad's car pulled up to the curb.

"Nooo!" Hailey croaked.

Sophie's spirits sagged like a week-old balloon. She scurried over to look under the car.

Just as Hailey did.

Whack! They bumped heads.

Sophie staggered backward.

Pulling off her glasses, Hailey eagle-screeched. "You bent them!"

Jordy flung the car door open. "Why did you throw Hailey's flashlight under our car, Sophie?"

"I didn't throw it. I tried to catch it. To be kind."

She wished she could jump on a swing, twirl herself around as far as possible in one direction, then let go. She'd spin so fast in the other direction, no one would know she was Sophie. Instead they'd think she was a tornado and run for their lives. No one would hang around to blame a tornado for things it didn't do on purpose.

Jordy's dad drove away.

Brayden came over to see Hailey's flashlight, Enoli at his side. "Aw, it's ruined," he said. Looking at it, Enoli covered her mouth.

"Don't pick it up," added Brayden. "There are too many cars pulling in."

Sophie nodded, then glanced in Hailey's direction. "You know, I didn't mean to bend your glasses."

"You should have let *me* get my flashlight back, Sophie," Hailey barked.

"I thought I was helping."

"It's wrecked, because of you." Hailey's

face tightened. "Just like my boots and my painting and Grandma's bloom and my glasses."

A baby-bird squeak rose from Sophie's throat. She rubbed her forehead, struggling to hold back the tears forming behind her eyes.

Brayden bit his lip. "Bad luck, Hailey."

"And Sophie made things worse," Hailey snapped.

"Not on purpose. She tried to catch your flashlight."

"Plus Sophie's forehead is sore," Enoli said, softly. "Where you bumped into her."

What? Brayden and Enoli are sticking up for me?

Hailey huffed. "What will I use for flashlight actions?"

Brayden tilted his head. "Miss Ruby's grey flashlight?"

"But mine was yellow, my favourite colour." Hailey sighed. "Everything's going wrong."

Sophie gazed at Hailey's sad face. She remembered being the new kid. *It must be hard on Hailey to have all of this happening. And just when she's starting at a new school.*

10

THE SCREAMING GIRL ON THE SLIDE

Sophie walked into the classroom and sat down.

Hailey took her seat seconds later. She stared gloomily at the bent glasses on her desk.

Touching the spot where Hailey's glasses rammed her forehead, Sophie winced. *Hailey, my never-ever-ever friend.*

She glanced outside. A crow perched

on the bar at the top of the slide. It bobbed its head, cawing at another crow standing in the wood chips below. Was the wood-chip crow getting blamed for stuff that wasn't its fault? Sophie felt like opening the window and cawing at the grumpy crow.

Miss Ruby faced the class. Her hair puff was flopping sideways. *So early? Something's wrong.*

Her teacher smiled sadly. "I'm sorry to say that Safiya is sick. She won't be at school today."

Everyone groaned.

"But she's the sun," Sophie cried. "Couldn't she skip the singing and just play her part?"

"She's dizzy, so I'm afraid not," answered Miss Ruby. "Yes, Brayden?"

"Standing onstage on the risers would be dangerous."

Enoli raised her hand. "She could fall."

Miss Ruby nodded. "We'll miss having Safiya play the sun. But I hear that one of you is quite the actor."

That's me. I love acting. Sophie grinned.

Sophie the sun-girl rose above her seat, her arms overhead like sunrays.

Bam! Her knees banged the underside of her desk.

The class roared with laughter.

"Are you all right?" asked Miss Ruby.

"Yes." Sophie plunked back into her seat, rubbing her legs, but smiling. "I think you have something exciting to tell me."

"I have something exciting to tell *everyone.*" Miss Ruby glanced one row over and two seats back. "Hailey, I hear you've acted in plays at a theatre."

Sophie glared at Hailey.

"That's right," Hailey answered. "Last Christmas, I played the part of the screaming girl on the slide behind Ralphie in *A Christmas Story*. And this year, I played Tessie the crybaby in *Annie*."

Miss Ruby I-care-smiled. "Can you take Safiya's place as the sun?"

"Sure." Hailey beamed.

Not me? Sophie squeezed her lips together end-of-toothpaste-tube tightly. *I played the part of the screaming girl on the slide last week. And I'm a crybaby whenever Auntie Pop-Pop serves turnips. Or squished squash.*

Wait. Sophie's lips softened. *I'm acting jealous because something nice happened to Hailey? She'll be a good sun. When she smiles, her face glows.*

Sophie pictured what her own face looked like a minute ago.

Thunderstorm eyebrows.

Squidward eyelids.

And grouchy-camel lips.

Erasing it all, she flashed a giant smile at Hailey.

Hailey's lips curled upward, then down again.

Is she trying not to smile? Sophie didn't have time to find out. Ideas were popping like movie-theatre popcorn in her head. Leaping up, Sophie asked Miss Ruby if she could speak with her in the hallway.

***

An hour later, Miss Ruby waved a bag at Sophie. "Your aunt brought everything you wanted from home." Miss Ruby went to Hailey's desk and whispered to her.

Grabbing her bent glasses, Hailey darted out the door and down the hallway.

With Auntie Pop-Pop.

And her mending kit.

Sophie crossed her fingers, her toes, and even her legs.

Would her plan work?

Minutes later, the class lined up for the assembly. "Flashlights in pockets, please." Miss Ruby led them to the gym.

Two Grade 5s stepped over to the microphone and told the students about upcoming events. Then Mr. Homework handed out some awards.

As the audience clapped, Sophie's class filed into the hallway. They scooted backstage past Brayden's mom as she helped Jordy into his costume.

The class climbed the stairs to the risers. Sophie and Brayden were in the top row, with Enoli below them. A sea of faces gazed at them from the gym floor.

Sophie glanced over her shoulder. Miss Ruby was staring down the hallway, wearing her worried-teacher look.

No Hailey, no sun.
No sun, no song.

11

HAILEY, NEVER-EVER-EVER FRIEND?

Where was Hailey? Sophie and her class fidgeted as they waited on the risers.

Suddenly, Hailey dashed backstage.

Wearing not-bent glasses.

Sophie grinned. *Yes! Auntie Pop-Pop fixed them. It's lucky she works at that glasses store.*

Brayden's mom helped Hailey into a padded costume bursting with sunrays.

Miss Ruby and her tower of hair hurried to the gym floor. She signalled to Mr. Homework.

The lights went out.

When the music began, the students sang about night and day, slanting their flashlights from low to high and high to low.

The chorus was next. Everyone oohed and aahed at the blinking, twinkling stars.

During the moon verse, Jordy climbed the stairs to the risers. He was wearing his moon mask and the headlamp Sophie lent him. The audience howled at Jordy— laughing at his toothy grin.

Seconds later, they let out ear-splitting squeals when the students shone their flashlights under their chins.

They repeated the chorus.

As they started the sun verse, the class shone wiggly sunrays overhead. Jordy the moon disappeared down the stairs on his side of the risers as Hailey the sun climbed the stairs on hers.

A spotlight blinked on above her. The audience let loose long, drawn-out gasps.

Hailey glowed.

Partly from the class's flashlights.

And partly from Sophie's dad's headlamp.

And Uncle Ray's headlamp.

And Auntie Pop-Pop's headlamp.

And Miss Ruby's turquoise flashlight in one hand.

And Sophie's zebra flashlight in her other hand.

And Sophie's cookie flashlight strung around her neck.

As the students sang about their friend the sun, they held their flashlights over their hearts. Sophie held Miss Ruby's grey one proudly.

The stage lights flicked on and the class chanted, "The sun has risen over Hilltop School. It's a new day!"

Wild clapping filled the gym. Hailey bowed.

Jordy returned to bow. He had moved Sophie's headlamp down and was wearing it over his mouth.

Everyone laughed.

My headlamp's covered in Jordy germs! Sophie imagined grinning, scruffy-legged bugs crawling across it. She wanted to stick out her tongue, but the audience was watching. She kept on smiling.

***

Sophie waited by the stage door. Most of the class had already left with Miss Ruby.

What would Hailey say when she walked out?

Jordy zipped into the hallway, still wearing his moon mask. He backward-walked up the hallway. "Thanks for lending me your headlamp, Sophie Trophy."

"I'm glad you wore it." Sophie's lips wriggled. "Except when you put it over your mouth."

"The audience went crazy." Jordy said. "I saw you pretending you didn't care."

"Oh, I cared, Light-Lips. You left Jordy germs on my headlamp!"

"I knew it. Jor-*dy*, Jor-*dy*, Jor-*dy*!" Arms raised in victory, he ran back to class.

Sophie chuckled.

Hailey, Brayden, and Enoli appeared. "You look like a yellow bouncy-ball in that costume, Hailey," squawked Brayden. Hailey and Enoli flung their heads back, laughing.

Listening to them, Sophie felt like a leftover doughnut. Still in the box.

Noticing Sophie, they stopped short. "We were just talking about you," Hailey said.

Sophie's stomach churned. *Just say you're my never-ever-ever friend, Hailey. Then I'll go hang out with the mushroom-eyed maple monster.*

She blinked. Was she imagining that great big smile on Hailey's face?

"You lent me your flashlight collection! *And* you used Miss Ruby's grey flashlight so I could borrow her turquoise one." Hailey hugged Sophie. "You're the best."

Sophie got all choked up. Like something was in her throat. A couple of hibernating turtles maybe? Or was it pure happiness?

Hailey grinned. "Thanks for asking your Auntie Pop-Pop to fix my glasses."

"That was awesome," said Brayden.

"Yes, great idea." Enoli patted Sophie's arm. Sophie got the best-friends feeling. "Thanks, guys."

Enoli and Brayden headed back to class.

Speaking softly, Hailey said, "I wasn't nice to you, Sophie. I acted worse and worse."

"You said everything's going wrong," whispered Sophie.

"Yes, since Grandma fell, my parents and I have to help her with everything. We're grumpy a lot. Mostly me."

"Sometimes Dad calls me a crabby critter," Sophie said. "When I don't wait my turn. Or I don't want to do all my homework. He helped me finish your grandma's letter."

"That letter made Grandma feel better," cried Hailey.

"She thinks you're wonderful. She

wants you to know the cactus is covered in blooms."

"Aww." Joy curled around Sophie's heart like fuzzy slippers around cold toes.

Hailey sighed. "Some things weren't your fault. They were Jordy's fault, or mine."

"But other stuff was my fault," Sophie said. "Sometimes I do the wrong thing."

"So do I," said Hailey. "I had a hard time staying mad at you because you're so funny."

Sophie rolled her eyes. "Sometimes I don't know I've said anything funny until someone laughs."

Hailey giggled. "Can you come over soon? Grandma wants to play Snap with us. She has old-fashioned cards with cute animals on them. The golden kitty is my favourite."

"Sure." Sophie's eyes sparkled. "I want

to meet your grandma. And the golden kitty."

Hailey grinned.

Sophie fought back a smile. "Brayden's wrong. You don't look like a bouncy-ball. You look like a duckling. Who swallowed pointy slices of pizza. And a stegosaurus."

Hailey laughed so hard she started slapping the wall.

Sophie headed back to class with Hailey, her truly-true friend.

ACKNOWLEDGEMENTS

As a teacher, I often saw students struggling like Sophie and Hailey to find their place socially at school. I longed to help them but knew that, for the most part, they needed to find their own way.

I based the layout of the school in my Sophie Trophy books on Ranch Park Elementary in Coquitlam, BC, having taught there for two decades (after teaching in Campbell River and Vancouver). This gives Ranch Park students the fun of recognizing their school as they read. The park in *Sophie Trophy Too* is based on Mariner Park next door, a park my classes and I loved.

A huge thank you to my long-time and much respected WriteOnFest colleagues Karen Autio, Loraine Kemp, Pat Fraser, and Mary Ann Thompson, who helped bring clarity to *Sophie Trophy Too* through their stellar critiquing skills. Thanks to Heather Conn, Debra Purdy Kong, and Port Moody's Kyle Centre writers' group for your excellent advice as you reviewed my chapters.

Thank you to illustrator Brooke Kerrigan. Readers often say that Sophie Trophy's big-eyed, caring gaze draws them to the book. Miss Ruby's towering hair puff has a pull of its own.

Thank you to my wonderful publisher, Melanie Jeffs of Crwth Press, for her guidance, enthusiasm, and insight into the development of my characters. Thank you also to Dawn Loewen for her top-notch copy editing, Audrey McClellan for her careful proof reading, and to Julia Breese for the appealing book layout and design.

As always, thank you to my dear husband, Wayne, for lightening my load in all the tiny ways that allow me more time for writing. Kelly, I feel fortunate to be able to question you about what works in a scene due to your excellent editing ability. Matthew, your unwavering belief in my books and support of my writing bring me joy.

ABOUT THE AUTHOR

Eileen Holland taught elementary school for thirty-three years and was often known as the funny teacher. Eileen has written dozens of magazine articles and served as Associate Western Editor of *The Landowner Magazine. Sophie Trophy Too* is her second novel. Eileen lives in Coquitlam, British Columbia, where she and her husband are kept busy by Sawyer, their water-crazy Nova Scotia Duck Tolling Retriever.

To learn more about Eileen and her writing, visit eileenhollandchildrensauthor.com.

ABOUT CRWTH PRESS

Crwth (pronounced crooth) Press is a small independent publisher based in British Columbia. A crwth is a Welsh stringed instrument that was commonly played in Wales until the mid-1800s, when it was replaced by the violin. We chose this word for the company name because we like the way music brings people together, and we want our press to do the same.

Crwth Press is committed to sustainability and accessibility. This book is printed in Canada on 100 percent post-consumer waste paper using only vegetable-based inks. For more on our sustainability model, visit www.crwth.ca.

To make our books accessible, we use fonts that individuals with dyslexia find easier to read. The font for this book is Lexie Readable.